HOP-A-LONG

Stories by LOYD TIREMAN
Adapted by EVELYN YRISARRI

Layout and Illustrations
By RALPH DOUGLASS

MESALAND
SERIES

A Facsimile of the 1944 First Edition

University of New Mexico Press   Albuquerque

20 19 18 17 16 15   1 2 3 4 5 6

LIBRARY OF CONGRESS CATALOGING-IN-PUBLICATION DATA

Tireman, L. S. (Loyd Spencer), 1896–1959, author.
  Hop-a-long / stories by Loyd Tireman ; adapted by Evelyn Yrisarri ;
layout and illustrations by Ralph Douglass.
    pages cm. — (Mesaland Series ; Book 2)
  "A facsimile of the 1944 first edition."
  Summary: "Follows the adventures of Hop-a-long, one of a litter of
four baby jackrabbits born in the early spring"— Provided by publisher.
  ISBN 978-0-8263-5608-6 (cloth : alk. paper) [1. Jackrabbits—Fiction.]
I. Yrisarri, Evelyn, adaptor. II. Douglass, Ralph, illustrator. III. Title.
  PZ7.T5167Ho 2015
  [E]—dc23
                        2015004441

JUMPING JACK

Hop-a-long was one of a litter of four baby jack rabbits born in the early spring. One night the bitter winter wind howled down from the north, and before morning all the baby rabbits, except two, were dead. These two were covered by the warm body of Mother Jack Rabbit and did not feel the cold wind. One of these was the Baby Jack we now know as Hop-a-long, the other was his sister.

Mother Jack told Cactus Jack, "Although

I have had dozens of babies in my lifetime,
never before have I had such a pretty baby as
this." She pointed to the rabbit that was all
gray except for a big white spot on one shoul-
der. This one had dainty feet, small ears, and
the most beautiful brown eyes imaginable.
From the time
she was
a few days old
this   or high,
little jack rabbit
liked to jump.
   She could not

jump very far   but

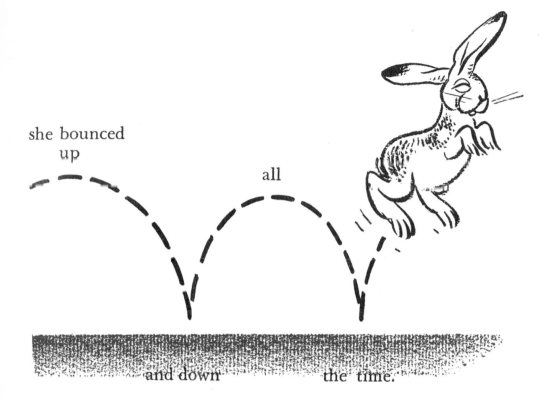

she bounced
up

all

and down   the time.

One black-tipped ear would be turned forward
with the other ear
laid back,

then she would give a jump
and flip
the other ear forward.

She was so cute and irresistible that they just naturally had to call her "Jumping Jack."

On the moonlight nights she liked to jump on the smooth sand beside the mesquite. She would jump in and out, back and forth, watching her shadow dance before her. In the late afternoon, Jumping Jack would watch the setting sun as it sank lower and lower behind

the mountain. As it disappeared, she would jump higher and higher trying to see how long she could watch the ball of fire.

Mother Jack loved Jumping Jack so much that she watched her lovely little rabbit all the time, always telling her,

> "You better watch your Ps and Qs
> For danger's always near.
> Eat only what you see me choose
> And then you need not fear."

Early that Spring came a warm rain lasting two days. The raindrops came drip, drip, dripping down. As the raindrops sank into the dusty earth they murmured to all the little seeds, "Wake up, wake up." Then the sunbeams whispered, "Come up, come up."

Each little seed stirred within the darkness of the pod and pushed tiny roots down into the brown, damp soil, searching for food.

Then the tiny leaves grew stronger, bursting the walls of their pods. As the warm sun continued to call, they pushed up and finally came out into the sunshine. A miracle happened! The dry, dusty, barren mesa became a beautiful garden of flowers. Here and there as far as one could see were little patches of color. Some were blue, some red, some yellow and white. In places the flowers were all mixed together like grandmother's old shawl.

Jumping Jack was enchanted. This was the most wonderful sight she had ever seen. She hopped from one patch to another looking at the different colors. She lay down and rolled, pretending she could feel the rich colors. Although desert flowers have little perfume, perhaps the dainty little rabbit could smell odors that others could not.

There was one particular flower that pleased her most of all. It was pinkish-white with little green leaves and not very tall. She rubbed and rubbed against it and finally took a little nibble. "Yum, yum," said little Jumping Jack. "This is delicious." So she ate all of it—the flower, the leaves, the branches right down to the root. Then she hunted and ate some more.

Hop-a-long was sitting under a chamiso bush watching the mesa when he saw Jumping Jack give a tremendously big jump. "She must be feeling very happy," thought Hop-a-long as he watched her. Jumping Jack continued to jump. She hopped side-ways, backwards, forwards, turned a somersault, then ran toward Hop-a-long. Her eyes were bulging and foam was on her lips. As she neared Hop-a-long she snapped at him. Hop-a-long turned and ran back to the mesquite thicket where Cactus Jack and Mother Jack were resting. "Come quickly!" he begged. "Something terrible is happening to Jumping Jack."

They all ran to the brow of the hill. Jumping Jack was now lying on the ground, quite still. "What happened, what did she do?" asked Mother Jack. "I don't know," said Hop-a-long, "She was rolling in the flowers, then she ate some pinkish-white flowers like this one." "Oh! my poor baby," cried Mother Jack. "That is a poisonous flower. I have told both of you to be careful and not eat strange plants."

"You'd better watch your Ps and Qs,
For death is always near,
And when you don't watch out, I lose
The ones so near and dear."

BIG FAT AND
LITTLE UGLY

Hop-a-long was out on the mesa prowling one day and chanced to go near the Prairie Dog Village. Two of his friends, Big Fat and Little Ugly, were sitting up very straight, quarreling. Hop-a-long sneaked up behind a bush to listen. Of course this was not the polite thing to do, but he did it anyway.

"If you wouldn't dig your home so close to mine, there would be more food for both of us," Big Fat was saying.

"That is true," replied Little Ugly, "and if you weren't so fat you could walk a few steps farther and find food."

"I know I'm fat, and that is the reason I don't like to get very far away from home. I run so slowly that Hungry Owl or Mister Coyote might catch me some day," said Big Fat. "I can feel Hungry Owl's claws in my back right now," - - and he popped down into his hole.

"Ho, ho," barked Little Ugly after him, "It was probably only a stub of grass tickling your fat sides."

Pretty soon Big Fat came out again, looking a wee bit sheepish, and said, "I guess I did get scared but someone is always trying to

catch me, I would make a delicious meal. Now you are all skin and bones and no one wants you."

"What a fibber you are," said Little Ugly very indignantly. "I --- ---," but he never finished, because Hop-a-long had moved a little. Little Ugly had seen the movement and dived into his hole. When he came out again he looked very carefully at the bush and saw it was only Hoppy. Little Ugly decided to have some fun, so he remarked very confidently to Big Fat, "There certainly are too many Jack Rabbits on the mesa this summer."

"That is right," said Big Fat. "There isn't enough food for all of us. Why don't they go farther away since they can run so much faster than we?"

"I think it's because they are afraid," said Little Ugly. "Remember that big Jack Rabbit called Hop-a-long that comes by here? Did you ever notice how skinny he is? His fur coat looks as though bugs had been in it—and afraid! Why, he jumps every time a meadow lark sings."

Big Fat didn't know Hop-a-long was within hearing. Being rather slow and easy going he

said, "Why Hop-a-long isn't such a bad fellow --- ---."

"No," interrupted Little Ugly, "he isn't bad, just stupid. He hasn't any manners, and isn't even polite. His long ears are always stretched --- ---."

Poor Hop-a-long was too ashamed to listen any longer. So he crept away as quietly as possible. He thought no one had seen him. But Little Ugly's eyes were very sharp and had seen Hoppy leave. Little Ugly and Big Fat had many laughs about Hoppy's listening. Whenever Hop-a-long came by after that, the prairie dogs would ask one another very innocently, "What do you think long ears were made for?"

HOP-A-LONG HURTS HIS FOOT

Jack rabbits do not have a nice new pair of shoes every month or two. No, Sir! They must grow their own shoes. On the bottom of each foot is a thick hard sole that protects the foot almost as well as the fancy shoes you buy. I said, "almost as well," for sometimes a rabbit does step on something that is sharp enough to hurt him.

One day Hop-a-long had been down to the alfalfa field. As he returned home, he felt very happy. The sky was blue and full of sunshine. The air was so clear he could see for miles. Hoppy forgot there were dangers and went hippity-hop over the mesa in long jumps. The mesa was such a pleasant place that he didn't watch where he was jumping. One front foot struck a spine of a Spanish bayonet bush. It jabbed right into his toe. My, oh my, how it hurt!

Hop-a-long sat down; held his foot off the ground and watched the blood drip into the sand. Soon it stopped bleeding. Then he put his foot down and stepped on it. Of course it hurt, but that couldn't be helped. So he went home.

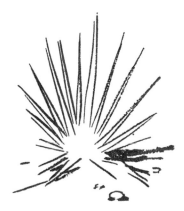

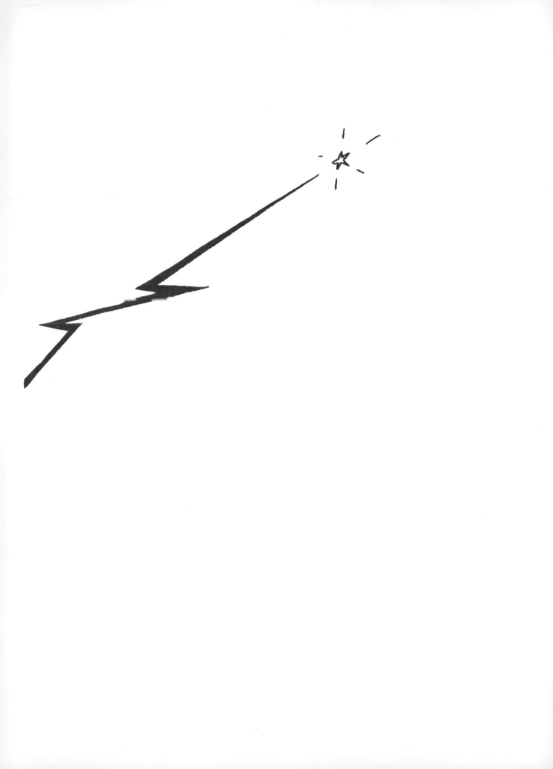

Mother Jack didn't have a clean white bandage to put on his foot to keep out the dirt, and the wound became infected. The foot became very sore and Hoppy could hardly step on it. He wasn't hungry now, but very thirsty. After a few days he became so hot and feverish that he knew

he must

go down

to the river

for a drink,

because he could not get enough water from the prickly pear cactus as he regularly did.

It was a long way to the river, especially when he had to go slowly. Hop-a-long watched very carefully for Coyotes. With a sore foot he wouldn't have much chance to escape, if one started to chase him.

At last he came to the river. As Hoppy

stooped to drink he happened to put his sore foot down into the mud. The mud was cool and felt good. Hop-a-long found a place under a bush where he could lie down and keep his foot in the mud. My, what a relief! Soon his hot feverish foot quit throbbing.

Once in a while he would drink but most of the time Hoppy just stayed right there in the moist dirt. This was good medicine and the sore foot gradually healed.

Perhaps that is why Hop-a-long always told his friends, "Look before you leap."

HOP-A-LONG GETS CAUGHT IN A SANDSTORM

The little breezes had been growing stronger all day. At first they whispered softly as they played in the sand, "Today is our day to play." Then after awhile they said, "Watch us grow stronger." Finally as the breezes filled the air with the sand they howled loudly and fiercely, "We've caught you-o-o-o."

Hop-a-long had noticed the wind growing stronger and stronger, but there was nothing he could do about it. He didn't have a hole to crawl into like the cotton-tails, kangaroo-rats, or the coyotes. Hoppy sat under a bush partly protected, but the wind began to whip the sand and dust around him. The day grew

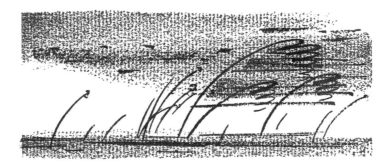

darker and darker. All he could see was the sun which looked like a big red ball through the dust.

One of the little breezes, which had grown to be a big big breeze now, flipped a pebble against Hop-a-long's back, and said, "Wake up fellow, don't go to sleep."

Hop-a-long gave a jump and since the bush was no longer any protection he began to hop slowly down the path with the wind. His eyes were full of sand; it settled in his ears and he could even taste it between his teeth. Hoppy didn't whine or complain. This had happened before and a little rabbit just had to endure it.

Through the dust he noticed the scent of

a man mixed with a gun smell. He couldn't see anything, but stumbled along. His nose soon told him that he was near the man and gun, so he turned off the path.

A hunter who had been caught in the storm was seated in a little arroyo. He was grumbling: "A fine thing! I can't see, and my gun is full of sand. Why did I come hunting today." Then he said some other words too, but I think they were bad words for the breezes snatched them up and carried them away before anyone heard them.

After a while Hop-a-long's nose told him that he was nearing a herd of sheep. This didn't frighten him. In such a sandstorm the herder and dogs would be too busy with the sheep to chase a jack rabbit. Soon Hoppy was among the sheep. He could just barely see them as they moved along with the storm. The dogs were trying to stop the sheep. It was easier to move with the storm than to stand still.

"Baa, baa-aa," the lambs were crying. The

wise old mother sheep answered, "Don't be afraid, this is only a little dust storm. After awhile the wind will blow itself away and we will be all right." "Where are we?" asked the lambs. "I don't exactly know, but do not fear, the herder and our friends, the dogs, are protecting us.

It seemed a very long time before the day was over and the storm passed. That night the stars came out very bright and clear. It seemed as though one could almost reach up and touch them. Hop-a-long could hear the

sheep as they lay down to rest. The herder was talking to his dogs, "I'm glad the sheep didn't run; you dogs did a good job." Somewhere near, a little bird twittered sleepily. Hop-a-long sat down under a bush and waited for the dawn.

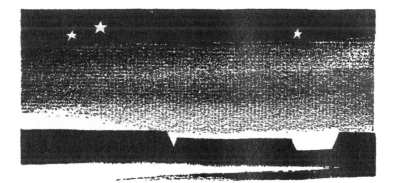

HOP-A-LONG'S FIRST SNOWSTORM

One dark, gloomy afternoon, late in the fall, Hop-a-long was hopping along the old trail toward the Mesquite Thicket. The clouds had looked like rain all day but Hoppy had not worried.

All of a sudden he noticed that the mountain had disappeared. Most astonishing! He sat down to think and scratched one ear. There seemed to be a white wall this side of the mountain. As he looked, the white wall moved toward him. It shut off his view of the Mesquite Thicket and came closer. He turned tail and began to run, but the whiteness soon overtook and surrounded him. It filled his eyes, it filled his ears, it was light but he couldn't see. He was so confused that he ran headlong into a piñon tree. Deep under the branches it was dry and free from snow. Hoppy crouched there in bewilderment. The strange whiteness hadn't harmed him, but he wasn't happy.

It snowed all night and he couldn't go home. During the storm the wind had drifted the snow. When morning came there was a snow bank a couple of feet high in front of Hoppy. After the storm had passed Hop-a-long decided

to start for home. He put his front feet on the edge of the snow bank and started to give a hop over it. Of course the soft snow could not hold his weight and in he fell, head first. Only his long hind legs stuck out. How they kicked, for Hoppy was scared nearly to death!

Being buried in the snow isn't fun, you know. Soon his kicking about brought him back into the clear space beneath the tree. He lay trembling and panting. He couldn't understand and we are apt to fear what we don't understand.

After awhile his courage returned and he hopped around to the other side of the tree. The drift was not so high there. He put one paw down on the snow and nothing happened. Then another paw, until he had moved away from the tree. In places the wind had swept the mesa clean of the snow. He wasn't completely happy but kept on going. As was his habit, he

paused by a bush to look around for any possible danger. Accidentally he brushed against a snow laden limb and down came the

snow on Hoppy's head. He jumped ten feet in his surprise and then shook the snow off his head. He looked to see where the enemy was that had played this trick. As he watched, he saw other piles of snow slide off limbs and understood what had happened.

Hopping along in the soft snow was fun. He would give great big hops and then look at his tracks. He really was a tremendous hopper, besides being very handsome. Hoppy approached the Mesquite Thicket. There was an arroyo just before the thicket and Hoppy thought to himself—"I'll just jump clear across and show the family what a real Jack Rabbit can do!"

He took a little run and gave a big jump. But again the snow fooled him. It had piled up on the opposite bank and instead of landing on firm ground, Hop-a-long hit the soft snow bank. Down he went, tumbling, tumbling into the snow.

Hop-a-long wasn't scared but his pride took a sudden tumble. He crawled out, covered with snow. His long ears were laid back as he slunk up the bank. He heard his uncle Black Jack say, "Yes, he is a fine jumper, but picks nice soft places to land."

HOP-A-LONG AND THE OWL

"Ho, hum," said Hop-a-long, stretching his long legs. "I'm tired of sitting here all day long. My legs hurt, and besides I want to go out and run and jump."

"That is perfectly natural," said Mother Jack Rabbit. "A young rabbit like you should run and play, but be careful. Hungry Owl

has been about lately, and she likes nothing better for supper than a nice young rabbit. Keep near bushes and trees and mind your Ps and Qs. If you see a moving shadow or hear a swish-swish of wings, jump for a bush as fast as you can."

"All right, Mom, I'll watch out for moving shadows and swishing wings."

It was a beautiful day and everything seemed just right. Hop-a-long kicked up his heels, laid his long ears back along his head and ran. He ran so fast down the hill that he looked like a long grey streak.

Suddenly he stopped short, just like that! He turned a couple of very fancy somersaults,

and danced around on his long hind legs. Oh, but it was grand to be alive!

Now Hop-a-long had been so active in the short time he had been playing that he became hungry. So he hopped away to find some tender leaves. As he slowed up to investigate a bug crawling along, something dark crossed his path, and zip! Hoppy jumped under a near-by juniper bush.

His heart went "bumpity bump." Still frightened, Hop-a-long peeped out from under the juniper bush. But he didn't hear any swish-swish of wings and nothing seemed to happen. Looking up, he saw the swaying branches of a tree. At once he knew there would be no swishing of wings for it was only the shadow of a tree.

Hoppy felt a little foolish as he crawled out from under the juniper bush and went gaily down the path.

After awhile he reached a mesquite bush and began nibbling a little of the sweet bark. He felt better in spite of his scare and went, lippity lip on his way. Again something dark and strange crossed his path. Zip! he jumped under a bush for the second time. Very carefully he looked about. The trees had stopped

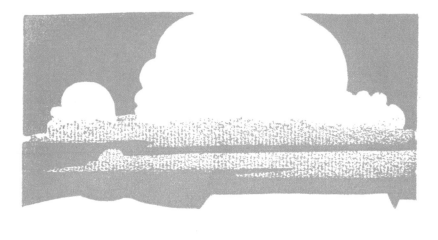

swaying. What could it have been? Looking up, he saw a large fleecy cloud drifting along.

By this time Hoppy was a little disgusted with himself for being so nervous and getting

fooled twice. The big red sun was almost out of sight. Hoppy decided to sit down on top of a little hill and look around. He knew this was dangerous, but nothing had happened so far. So Hoppy no longer felt that he should be careful. Foolish little Hoppy sat on top of the hill, in plain sight of everything!

If Hop-a-long had been very alert and had looked very carefully, he would have noticed that just a short distance away, in a juniper bush, on a near-by hill, sat Hungry Owl. Hungry Owl had just awakened from a nap. She was thinking very seriously of hunting her supper. Her round yellow eyes opened and shut slowly. Then she saw Hoppy sitting up straight and unafraid on the hill.

Hungry Owl fluffed herself up like a big brown ball. Flapping her wings several times she flew straight toward Hoppy. Poor little Hoppy! Poor foolish little Hoppy! He heard the sound of those strong wings. Then he

realized how foolish it
had been to sit up
straight and unafraid on
the top of the hill.
For half a second he
did not know just what
to do. That terrible
swish-swish of wings was
almost upon him. He
knew that he must do
something and do it in
a great big hurry.
Hoppy did the first
thing that popped into
his head. He just jumped

as far and as quickly as
he could. It was mighty
lucky that he was such a
good jumper. For just at
that very minute the owl
sailed over the place
where he had been sit-
ting. Hoppy heard the
clicking of her sharp
claws, and the screeching
of her anger at having
missed such a choice
supper for herself and
her little hungry babies.
Old Hungry Owl flew
back and forth trying to
see Hoppy. But he was
hiding under a tangle of
thorny bushes. Hoppy

sat very still, and as he sat there in the safety of
the bushes, he thought:

"When the sun is going down,
And the stars are coming out,
You'd better mind your Ps and Qs
When Old Hungry Owl's about."

swaying. What could it have been? Looking
up, he saw a large fleecy cloud drifting along.

By this time Hoppy was a little disgusted
with himself for being so nervous and getting

fooled twice. The big red sun was almost out of sight. Hoppy decided to sit down on top of a little hill and look around. He knew this was dangerous, but nothing had happened so far. So Hoppy no longer felt that he should be careful. Foolish little Hoppy sat on top of the hill, in plain sight of everything!

realized how foolish it
had been to sit up
straight and unafraid on
the top of the hill.
For half a second he
did not know just what
to do. That terrible
swish-swish of wings was
almost upon him. He
knew that he must do
something and do it in
a great big hurry.
Hoppy did the first
thing that popped into
his head. He just jumped

If Hop-a-long had been very alert and had looked very carefully, he would have noticed that just a short distance away, in a juniper bush, on a near-by hill, sat Hungry Owl. Hungry Owl had just awakened from a nap. She was thinking very seriously of hunting her supper. Her round yellow eyes opened and shut slowly. Then she saw Hoppy sitting up straight and unafraid on the hill.

Hungry Owl fluffed herself up like a big brown ball. Flapping her wings several times she flew straight toward Hoppy. Poor little Hoppy! Poor foolish little Hoppy! He heard the sound of those strong wings. Then he